Transformers: Revenge of the Fallen: When Robots Attack!
HASBRO and its logo, TRANSFORMERS, the logo and all related characters
are trademarks of Hasbro and are used with permission. © 2009 Hasbro. All Rights Reserved.
© 2009 DreamWorks, LLC and Paramount Pictures Corporation. All Rights Reserved.
Printed in the United States of America.
No part of this book may be used or reproduced in any manner whatsoever without written
permission except in the case of brief quotations embodied in critical articles and reviews.
For information address HarperCollins Children's Books,
a division of HarperCollins Publishers, 10 East 53rd Street, New York, NY 10022.
www.harpercollinschildrens.com

Library of Congress catalog card number: 2008940051
ISBN 978-0-06-172965-2
Book design by John Sazaklis
09 10 11 12 13   UG   10 9 8 7 6 5 4 3 2 1
❖
First Edition

TRANS FORMERS
REVENGE OF THE FALLEN

WHEN ROBOTS ATTACK!

Adapted by Ray Santos

Illustrated by MADA Design, Inc.

Digital colors by Kanila Tripp

Based on the Screenplay by

Ehren Kruger & Alex Kurtzman & Roberto Orci

HarperEntertainment
An Imprint of HarperCollinsPublishers

Two years ago, Sam Witwicky's life changed forever when his first car turned into a giant robot named Bumblebee. He was part of an alien race called Transformers, who had come to Earth looking for the AllSpark.

The AllSpark cube was the source of the alien life and could create Transformers from regular mechanical objects.

The evil Decepticons tried to use the AllSpark to rule the Earth, but Sam and his friends the Autobots fought back. Sam smashed the AllSpark into the Decepticon leader's chest, destroying both.

Things eventually returned to normal for Sam—if having a Transformer for a car was normal! Now Sam was packing for his next adventure: college.

"Look what I found!" said Sam's mom. "Your baby booties!"

"We're both real proud of you, kiddo," said his dad. "You're the first Witwicky to go to college!"

Sam groaned and handed his dad a box to put in the car.

Up in his room, Sam sorted through a pile of clothes. He found the shirt he was wearing the day he had saved the world by destroying the AllSpark.

Or at least he thought the AllSpark had been destroyed. When Sam held up the shirt, a tiny sliver fell out of the pocket!

Sam tried to catch the piece of AllSpark, but its powerful energy gave him a shock. Sam dropped the sliver on the floor, and it quickly burned a hole all the way down to the kitchen. The electric outlets in the walls began to spark.

Sam's touch had activated the AllSpark, and Sam knew that even a small piece had enough power to create an army of evil robots. He had to destroy it!

In the kitchen, the AllSpark bounced off the counter with a burst of energy. Suddenly, all the appliances came to life. They were all changed into robots!

The cappuccino maker started shooting fireballs across the room. The garbage disposal used its sawlike blades to shred its way out of the metal sink. The microwave, electric mixer, and the blender all jerked to life!

In Sam's room, the sparking outlets had started a fire. He poured a bottle of water over the flames, but water doesn't put out electrical fires. It just drained through the hole in the floor!

In the kitchen, the blender noticed the water dripping down from the ceiling. Water could short out the small robots! The blender ordered the other 'bots to march upstairs and find the source. The cappuccino maker left a trail of coffee on the floor.

Sam's dad came into the kitchen, but he didn't notice that all the appliances were gone. All he saw were the brown stains on the floor.

"Honey!" he called to Sam's mom. "I think the dog's started drinking cappuccino!"

In his room, Sam heard his dad's voice. *Oh, no!* He had to get his parents out of the house until he got the situation under control!

Sam tried to leave his room, but a tower of robots had already reached the doorknob . . . and they were coming in!

The appliances swarmed into the room. All of them had parts that had changed into horrible weapons. An egg beater hit Sam in the knees, and then the mixer started firing. Metal pellets hit the fish tank. Water splashed everywhere!

Sam hid behind his desk and looked around, but the only way to escape was through the window.

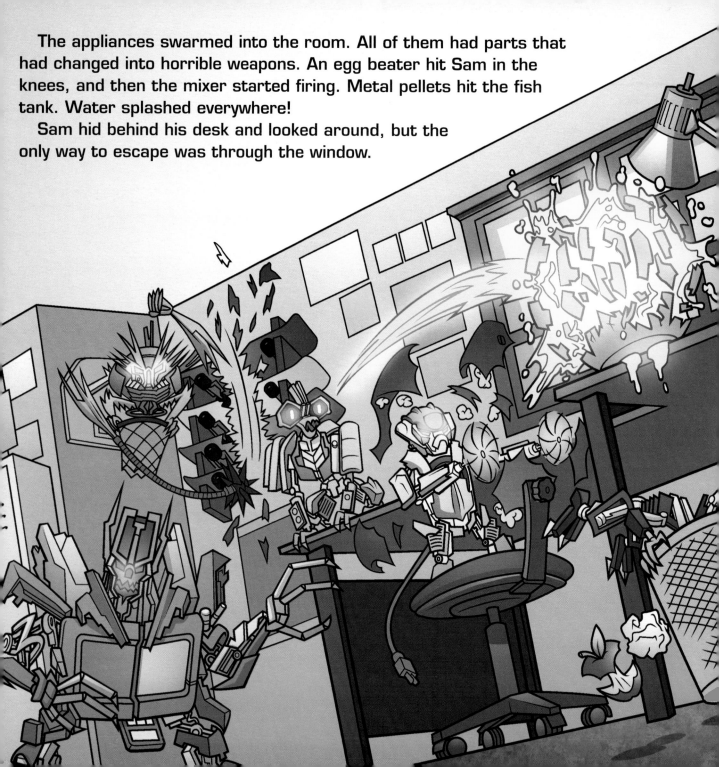

Sam climbed out of the window and tumbled to the ground. Luckily, there were some bushes to break his fall. As Sam landed with a loud thud, his dad came out into the backyard. "What's all the racket?" he yelled.

The electric mixer 'bot looked out the bedroom window. Its arms turned into rocket launchers and started firing missiles.

"Dad! Take cover!" Sam called as the doghouse behind them exploded.

"BUMBLEBEE!" yelled Sam. The yellow car with black racing stripes crashed through the wall of their garage and screeched to a stop in front of Sam.

The Camaro quickly changed into a giant robot.

The small home appliances were no match for Bumblebee. He was able to destroy the renegade robots with a few quick blasts from his plasma cannon.

The only problem was that Bumblebee also completely destroyed Sam's house!

Sam was relieved that the battle was over, but his mom was very upset. She turned to Bumblebee and yelled, "My house! I want that talking alien car out of here!" Bumblebee knew that he was in trouble, but he didn't mind. He had done his job protecting Sam, and the family was safe again!